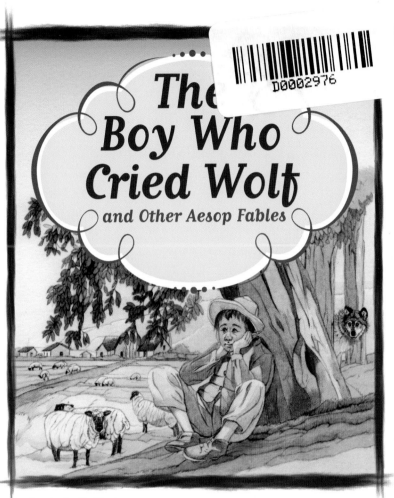

The Boy Who Cried Wolf
and Other Aesop Fables

Lee Aucoin, *Creative Director*
Jamey Acosta, *Senior Editor*
Heidi Fiedler, *Editor*
Produced and designed by
Denise Ryan & Associates
Illustration © Patrizia Donaera
Rachelle Cracchiolo, *Publisher*

Teacher Created Materials

5301 Oceanus Drive
Huntington Beach, CA 92649-1030
http://www.tcmpub.com
Paperback: ISBN: 978-1-4333-5648-3
Library Binding: ISBN: 978-1-4807-1747-3
© 2014 Teacher Created Materials
Printed in China
Nordica.042019.CA21900329

**Retold by
Leah Osei**

**Illustrated by
Patrizia Donaera**

2

Contents

4

Foreword

· · ● ● ·

Aesop's fables are among the oldest stories in the world. No one knows who Aesop was, although it is thought he was a slave who lived in ancient Greece. The stories he told were not written down until about two hundred years later. They were written in Greek and Latin first and then later in English.

The Boy Who Cried Wolf

Once there was a boy who had to look after a flock of sheep every day as they grazed near a village. One day, it was raining and the boy was bored, so he decided to play a trick on the villagers.

"Wolf! Wolf!" he shouted as loudly as possible. "A wolf is attacking the sheep!"

The villagers immediately ran to where the sheep were grazing. They ran as fast as the wind to drive away the wolf.

When they rushed to the field and found the sheep were quite safe, the boy laughed and laughed. The villagers did not find it funny.

The next day, the boy shouted as loudly as possible, "Wolf! Wolf! A wolf is attacking the sheep!"

The villagers ran to the field as fast as the wind. Again, they found the sheep were safely grazing on the lush green grass. The boy laughed more than ever, but the villagers found it even less funny.

On the third day, a wolf really did come. "Wolf! Wolf!" shouted the boy as the sheep ran in all directions, trying to escape from the wolf.

"Oh, please, come quickly!" the boy cried. But none of the villagers took any notice of his cries. No one ran to the field because they thought the boy was playing tricks, just as he had done before.

If you tell lies, no one will believe you when you tell the truth.

The Wolf and His Shadow

One winter's evening, the wolf noticed his shadow, which looked enormous in the light of the setting sun.

"Why, that's *my* shadow," said the wolf. "How big I am! Not even the lion is as big as that. The lion calls himself King of the Animals, but I shall be the king from now on."

So, the wolf strutted about, planning what he would do as king, noticing nothing around him.

Suddenly, the lion sprang on him and swallowed him whole!

After the lion licked his lips, he said, "What a silly wolf! Everyone knows that the size of your shadow changes depending on the time of the day."

Don't let your imagination run away with you.

Zeus and the Jackdaw

The Greek god Zeus once decided to name the King of the Birds. He called all the birds before him so that he could decide which bird was the most beautiful.

The jackdaw looked into the lake and saw how ugly he was. But he wanted to be the King of the Birds. So he searched around and found feathers that had fallen from other birds. He dressed himself in this feathered finery and presented himself to Zeus. No bird was more colorful than he.

Zeus declared him to be the most beautiful, naming him the King of the Birds. But the other birds were not fooled—they recognized their feathers and, one by one, reclaimed them.

Soon, the jackdaw was shown to be nothing but what he was. He was not the King of Birds, just a plain jackdaw.

Don't pretend to be someone you aren't.

The Mouse and the Lion

One day, when a lion was stretched out on the ground asleep, a plucky mouse began to run up and down his muzzle. The lion soon woke. He reached out his giant paw, snatched up the mouse, and prepared to devour her.

"Oh, I beg your pardon," said the mouse. "Please spare me, and one day, I may be able to help you."

The lion was so amused by the idea of this small creature being able to help him that he laughed and let the mouse go.

A few days later, some hunters caught the lion and tied him to a tree. Then, they went to fetch their wagon to take the lion away.

The lion roared, and the little mouse he had chosen not to eat heard him. She saw his plight and called her friends. Together, they gnawed the lion free of his bonds.

Even the weak and small can help the big and mighty.

The Grasshopper and the Ants

One cool winter's day, when the sun came out unexpectedly, all the ants hurried from their anthill and began to spread out their grain to dry. All summer long, they had worked to collect it.

A grasshopper appeared. He looked at what the ants were doing and said, "I am so hungry. Please, will you give me some of your grain?"

One of the ants stopped working for a moment to reply, "Why should we give you our grain? Where is your own food for the winter?"

"I have none," said the grasshopper. "I had no time to work and collect food during the summer. I was too busy singing."

The ants laughed. "If you spent the summer singing, you will have to spend the winter dancing for your supper," they said.

And the grasshopper went on his way—hungry.

Being lazy seems like fun, but hard work brings rewards.

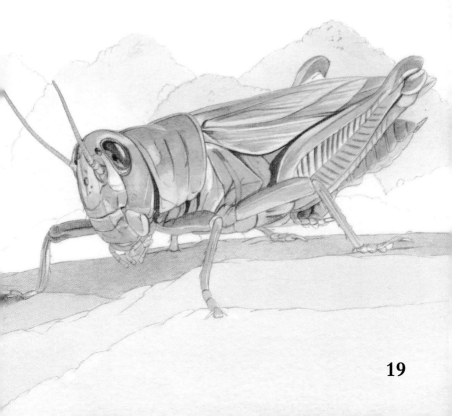

The Fat Hens and the Thin Hens

Once, many hens lived together in a farmyard. Some were very fat, but others were thin and scrawny.

The fat hens laughed at the thin ones and called them rude names, such as "Thinnie Winnie," "Lean Lizzie," "Scraggy Aggie," and "Skinny Banana Toes."

One day, the cook was asked to prepare roasted chicken for dinner because a large number of people were coming for supper. When the cook went out into the farmyard, the hens looked up to see which ones she would choose.

The cook selected all the fat hens. The skinny ones laughed now!

Don't laugh at the unfortunate: They may turn out to be luckier than you.

The Wolf and the Heron

One day, a wolf got a bone stuck in his throat. It hurt so much that he went looking for someone to take it out. By and by, he met a heron.

The heron had a long neck and a long, pointed beak. The wolf knew this was just the thing to pick out the bone. The wolf politely asked the heron whether she would help him.

The heron stopped and thought for a moment. "What will you give me if I put my head in your mouth?"

"I'll give you a big reward," croaked the wolf.

So, the heron put her head inside the wolf's mouth and gently pulled the bone from his throat. The wolf, now feeling much better, thanked the heron and went on his way.

"Hey!" called the heron. "Where's my reward?"

23

"Oh, you got it," replied the wolf. "From now on, you can boast to everyone that you put your head inside a wolf's mouth and lived to tell the tale."

Don't expect to be rewarded for helping the wicked.

The Crab and His Mother

"Why are you walking sideways?" a mother crab asked her baby. "You should walk straight."

"I'm only copying you," said the little crab. "If you show me how, I will walk straight."

But the mother crab only knew how to walk sideways, so the crabs went on as before.

If you can't lead by example, don't tell others how to act.

The Wolf in Sheep's Clothing

There was once a wolf who tried time and again to steal a sheep, but the shepherd looked after his sheep so well that he drove the wolf away every time he appeared.

One day, the wolf had an idea. He stole a fleece that had been sheared from one of the sheep and pulled it over his back. Then, the wolf strolled into the field as if he were returning home.

No one recognized him for what he was. The wolf lunged at the fattest sheep he could find, opening his jaws to seize it by the throat. Suddenly, he heard a voice behind him. "Now, which of these sheep is fat enough for me to eat?" said the shepherd.

Licking his lips, the shepherd spotted his supper. Then, picking up the wolf, the shepherd carried him off to eat for his evening meal.

Appearances are often deceiving.

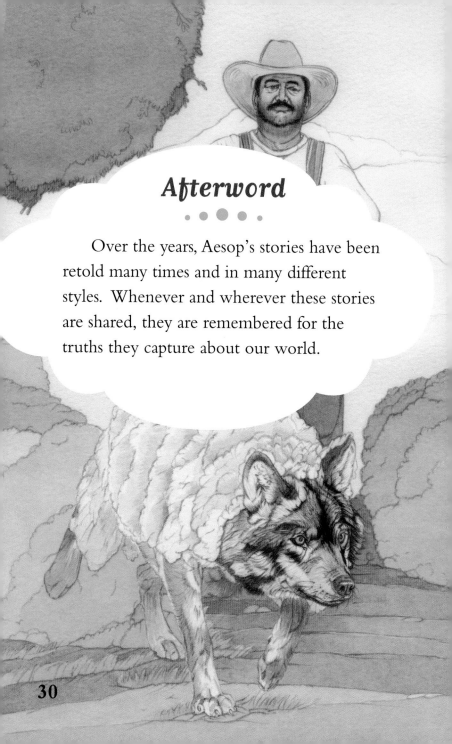

Afterword

• • • •

Over the years, Aesop's stories have been retold many times and in many different styles. Whenever and wherever these stories are shared, they are remembered for the truths they capture about our world.

Leah Osei lives in Victoria, Australia. Leah still has her first book of Aesop's fables, which is now very worn and tattered. So that she can protect it, she has at least four other collections of Aesop's fables in her very large library of children's picture books! When asked what her favorite Aesop tale is, she always says, "The Boy Who Cried Wolf."

Patrizia Donaera lives in Savona, Italy. Soon after Patrizia gained an illustration degree at Milan's Istituto Europeo di Design, she began working with French and English publishing houses. Her work usually is created using watercolor and colored pencils, although she does make some digital illustration.